THE SESAME STREET
TREASURY

Featuring Jim Henson's Sesame Street Muppets

VOLUME 3

STARRING
THE NUMBER
3
AND THE LETTER
C

Children's Television Workshop/Funk & Wagnalls, Inc.

WRITTEN BY:
Dina Anastasio
Linda Bove with
the National Theatre of the Deaf
Michael Frith
Emily Perl Kingsley
Sharon Lerner
Jeffrey Moss
Norman Stiles
Ellen Weiss
Dan Wilcox

ILLUSTRATED BY:
Art-so-fine
Tom Cooke
Peter Cross
Larry DiFiori
Mary Grace Eubank
Michael Frith
Joe Mathieu
Kelly Oechsli
Michael J. Smollin
Daniel Wilcox

PHOTOGRAPHS BY:
Neil Selkirk
View-Master International Group

A Colorful Tale

One cold, winter morning Bert and Ernie and Grover had nothing to do.

"I wish it were summer," said Ernie. "Then we could go swimming."

"And we could play in the park," said Bert.

"If it were summer, I, Grover, would ride my bike," said Grover.

"I know," said Ernie. "Let's draw a picture of what it's like in the summer."

Bert hung a large piece of paper on the wall. Then Ernie and Bert and Grover took out their pencils and drew a picture of the sky, the trees, the flowers, and the sun. Ernie drew some round things on his tree.

When they were finished Ernie said, "That doesn't look like summer. In the summer the trees are green, and the flowers are red and yellow. There isn't any color in our picture."

He opened a drawer and took out some crayons. "I only have four crayons," he said. "I have a red one, a blue one, a yellow one, and a green one."

"That's all we need," said Bert. And he started to color the sky blue.

"I, Grover, will color the grass and the trees," said Grover. And he colored the grass and the trees green.

"And I'll color the sun," said Ernie, picking up the yellow crayon.

When they were finished, Bert and Ernie and Grover colored the flowers red and yellow.

Then they stood back and looked at their picture of summer.

"Oh, no!" said Grover. "This is not right. We did not color the round things that are growing on Ernie's tree."

"They're oranges," said Ernie. "And we can't color them. We don't have an orange crayon."

"I, Grover, know just what to do," said Grover. "I will color them yellow and it will be a banana tree." And he colored the round things yellow.

"That's silly," said Bert. "Bananas aren't round. They're long and skinny. I know, we can color them red and say it's an apple tree."

"It's my tree," said Ernie, "and I say

they're oranges."

"But we don't have an orange crayon," said Bert. "Apples are round, and if we color them red, it will be an apple tree." And he colored the round things red.

Bert and Ernie and Grover looked at the round things and they started to laugh.

"How do you like that," said Bert. "When you mix yellow and red, you get........."

"ORANGE!" shouted Grover.

"You see," said Ernie. "I told you it was an orange tree!"

Oscar the Grouch

Home:	Trash Can, 123 Sesame Street
Favorite Food:	Sardine and spinach sundae
Favorite Drink:	Pickle juice
Best Friend:	Grungetta Grouch
Favorite Pet:	Slimey the Worm
Favorite Activities:	Disagreeable Order of Grouches meetings, writing for <u>The Daily Grouch</u> newspaper, reporting on WORM-TV
Favorite Vacation:	Two weeks at the Mudville City Dump
Favorite Weather:	Cold and nasty, gray sky, with occasional rain and sleet
Pet Peeve:	Cheerful friends
Favorite Saying:	"Have a yucchy day."

The Count Goes "C" Shopping

The Count looked out his window and frowned. "Cloudy," he muttered. "How boring." He squinted up at a cloud right above him.

"Just a minute!" he said suddenly. "What's this? A cloud that looks like the letter C! That gives me a wonderful idea: I'll count C words today! Oh, joy! You see, every cloud has a silver lining."

"I'll just begin my C counting in my cupboard," he thought to himself. But all he found in the cupboard was one can of cat food. "One," he said. "One can of cat food. I need more C words to count!"

The Count decided to go to the supermarket. When he got there, he went straight to the fruits and vegetables.

"Let me see," he said. "Ah, yes, carrots. That's one lovely C word. Oh, and look at this—cabbage! I love it! Two C foods in my shopping cart!" Then he took some corn, some cranberries, a stalk of celery, and a lot of cauliflower. Then he rushed on, feeling very happy indeed. Already he had seven C foods in his cart!

The Count rammed his cart into a big stack of soup cans. "Oops!" he said. "That was a big mistake. But look at all those nice cans on the floor. I'd better count them!"

Next the Count headed for the spice rack. "Wonderful!" he exclaimed. "Lots of C things here, too, and they smell so good. Cinnamon! Cloves! Caraway! I'll take them all!"

Then he thought, "Maybe something sweet would be nice. Yes, here we are. Candy canes! Wonderful carrot cakes! And crunchy cookies!"

The Count's cart was getting full. He whizzed up and down the aisles, grabbing things and tossing them into his cart.

"Cider!

"Crackers!

"Crab cakes! Oh, joy!"

Finally his cart was so full that he couldn't get another C thing in it.

The storekeeper looked at the Count's shopping cart in disbelief. "That's going to cost you a lot of money," he said. "Are you sure you want to buy all those things?"

"Buy them?" repeated the Count. "Who said I wanted to buy them? I just wanted to count them. Seventy-three wonderful C foods in my shopping cart!

"I'll just buy a quart of milk and some eggs, please." The Count took his small bag of groceries and counted the steps back to his castle.

The storekeeper, shaking his head, hung a sign on the door and muttered, "Here's another C word!"

CLOSED

Fall

The Count loves counting leaves as they gently float down.
He loves counting colors—"Green, red, yellow, brown!"
Days grow shorter and nighttime brings freezes.
Bert's kite cannot fight strong autumn breezes.

Grover swoops and loops on his cute roller skates;
For Halloween and Thanksgiving he joyfully waits.
Betty Lou on her bike is in a big hurry,
For summer is over. Soon snowflakes will flurry.

Three Monster Catch

Grover and Cookie Monster were playing catch. Herry Monster walked over to Grover and Cookie. "Can I play ball with you?" Herry Monster asked.

"Oh, that is a good idea," Grover said. "We will play Three Monster Catch. We will stand in a circle and throw the ball to each other. First I throw the ball to Cookie. Then Cookie throws the ball to Herry. Then Herry throws the ball to me. Won't that be fun? First, I Grover, will throw the ball to Cookie Monster." Grover threw the ball to Cookie. Cookie Monster caught the ball.

"Next, me, Cookie Monster, will eat the ball," said Cookie.

"No! No!" said Grover. "Don't eat the ball! Throw it to Herry Monster."

"Yes, me know," said Cookie. "Me only kidding." So Cookie Monster threw the ball to Herry. But Herry did not put his hands out to catch it. The ball landed on the ground.

"Stop the game!" said Grover. "What is the matter, Herry? You forgot to catch the ball."

Herry looked very sad. "I didn't forget, Grover," said Herry. "I .... I don't know how to catch a ball." And Herry started to cry.

"Don't cry, Herry," said Grover. "Cookie and I will teach you how to catch."

"You will?" sobbed Herry. "Gee, that's great."

Grover and Cookie showed Herry how to hold his hands together in front of his body to catch the ball. Then Cookie threw Herry the ball. But the ball bounced right out of Herry's hands.

"Herry, my good friend," Grover said, "you have to hold the ball tightly when it lands in your hands. Try again." So Herry tried again. Grover threw him the ball. This time it bounced off Herry's chest.

"Look at ball, Herry," Cookie explained, "don't look at your hands. You see ball coming, then move hands to catch it."

"Oh, I'll never learn how to catch!" said Herry. "I'm going home. You two play without me."

"Hold it, Her--ry!" said Grover. "Do not give up. I had to practice two weeks before I could catch a ball. Now, try again."

Catch it!

So Cookie and Grover kept throwing the ball to Herry. Soon, he was able to catch it.

"Now," Grover said, "we can all catch, so let us play Three Monster Catch."

Just as they were about to start playing, Big Bird came along. "Hi, everybody!" he said. "Can I play, too?"

"Sure," said Herry. "Here, catch the ball." And he threw the ball to Big Bird.

"But I don't know how to catch," said Big Bird.

"You don't ?" said Herry. "Well, Big Bird, take it from me—all you need is a little practice. I will teach you how to catch the ball."

So Herry Monster taught Big Bird how to catch the ball, and they all played Three Monster and One Bird Catch until it was time to go home.

c C A Poem by Cookie Monster

C is for COOKIES.
Me like them a bunch.
Me crunch them for dinner
And breakfast and lunch.

And then there are CRUMBS.
Cookie crumbs are so yummy!
Me sweep them off table
And into my tummy.

Did you know
the word CARTON
begins with a C?
That's the box
cookies come in.
It tastes good to me!

Well, that's all the C words
Me got for today.
Me get in my car now
And me drive away.

Hey, wait!

The word CAR starts with C.
Boy, that's neat!
Me thought me had run out of
C things to eat.

CRUNCH!

CRUNCH!

CRUNCH!

Tasty—
But not as good as
COOKIE!

Bye-bye!

Crafts for All Seasons

Spring

Hello, everybodee! This is Old Farmer Grover here. It is springtime, and spring is the time when all the pretty flowers bloom. I will show you how to make some flowers of your own.

Get some paper cups, some straws, some paste, and some paper and crayons. Draw some BEAUTIFUL flowers on the paper, cut them out, and stick them to the straws. Then put some sand in the cups and stick the straws in the sand. AREN'T THEY BEAUTIFUL?

You can even decorate the cups, like I did.

Use Paste or Tape

Summer

You know what us Grouches like to do in the summer? We like to go down to the *swamp* and play in the MUD. Here are some of my favorite MUD toys...

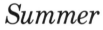

The best thing to use is a plastic bleach bottle. You can cut off the bottom, and use it for a pail.

And you can cut the top, like this...and it makes a super-dooper *mud* scooper.

Of course, if you're not a grouch you can use them at the beach for SAND toys...
...........BLECCH!

KNEE DEEP!

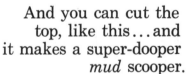

Fall

Hi, I'm Betty Lou. When the fall winds blow, I love to make pretty pinwheels and watch them spin. First, take a square piece of paper and color it with bright designs on both sides.

Then fold it in half, like this...

and then again, like this...

Now draw a small circle right in the middle of the paper. Cut on the fold lines toward the middle, until you reach the outside of your circle. BE SURE you don't cut all the way through the middle.

Now take one corner of each triangle and stick it to your middle circle like this...

Last of all, take a pin and a straw, and stick the pin through the middle of the pinwheel and through the straw.

(Stick a piece of cork or the eraser from a pencil on the pin so you won't get pricked.)

Now you can take your pinwheel out for a spin.

Winter

Oh, dear! It's getting cold. It must be winter. Do you know what I love about the winter? All the beautiful snowflakes. I'll show you how to make some. All you need is some white paper squares and a pair of scissors.

First fold your paper in half. Then fold it in half again... and then fold it one MORE time, into a triangle.

Now snip out bits from each side of the triangle.

Be sure to leave some space between each snip.

You can make all different kinds of snowflakes to hang on your walls and windows. Isn't that nice?

ROPA   CLOTHING

Say it in Spanish!

impermeable
raincoat

guantes
gloves

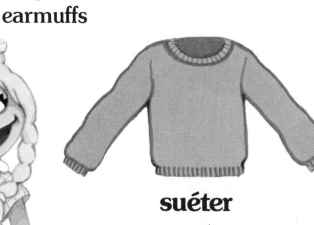

abrigo
coat

orejeras
earmuffs

botas de goma
rubber boots

suéter
sweater

zapatos
shoes

cinturón
belt

pantalones interiores
underpants

pantalones
pants

falda
skirt

camisa
shirt

pijama
pajamas

chinelas
slippers

vestido
dress

camiseta
T-shirt

gorra
cap

medias
socks

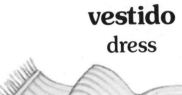

bufanda
scarf

Prairie Dawn was playing with her toy cars.

"The red car is driving this way," she said. "The blue car is driving that way. The yellow car is headed here. And the green car is headed there." Then Prairie Dawn smiled happily. "It's lucky that these cars aren't real! There's no traffic light on this table!"

colors

Colors

red

blue

yellow

green

squeeze fist

orange

white

black

purple

pink

brown

The Monster's Three Wishes

Once there lived a little monster
In a kingdom far away.
And a very strange thing happened
As he brushed his teeth one day.

As he squeezed his tube of toothpaste,
Deepest thunder shook the skies.
And suddenly a genie stood
Before his very eyes.

"I'm the genie of the toothpaste,"
Said the genie with a laugh.
"I've been trapped inside
             that toothpaste tube
For **3** weeks and a half.
You squeezed the tube and set me free
So here is what I'll do—
I'll let you have **3** wishes
And I'll make them all come true."

"Oh boy!" exclaimed the monster,
"Wow! **3** wishes just for me!
Now let me think and then decide
What my first wish will be."

Now my favorite thing is cookies,
Thought the monster with a grin.
But first I'll wish for something nice
To keep my cookies in.
I would like a million cookies,
But before I use that wish...

"Hey, Genie," said the monster,
"Will you please bring me a <u>dish</u>?"

"Will I ever!" said the genie,
"For your wish is my command."
And instantly a dish appeared
Right in the monster's hand.

"Hey, I did it!" cried the genie.
"Wow! I haven't lost my touch!"
"It's a nice dish," said the monster,
"But it won't hold very much."

The monster thought of all the cookies
That he'd soon get with his wish.
And he knew a million cookies
Couldn't fit on one small dish.

He would need something much bigger.
So the monster said, "Hey, Genie!
I would like a great big box ...
This plate is much too teeny!"

"You want a box? You've got it,"
Said the genie with a smirk.
And instantly a box appeared.
The monster cried, "Nice work!"

But although the box was pretty big
And could hold lots of stuff—
Could it hold a million cookies…?
It just wasn't big enough.

So the monster called the genie
And said, "Boy, am I in luck!
Since you'll give me what I wish for…
How about a great big <u>truck</u>?"

And right away a truck appeared
Before the monster's eyes.
"Fantastic!" cried the monster.
"It is just the perfect size!"

"It will hold a million cookies,
And I'll never have to worry.
And that is what I wish for!
Give me cookies now! Please hurry!"

"I am sorry," said the genie,
"For though cookies are delicious,
I *cannot* give them to you
'Cause you've used up your **3** wishes."

"Oh, no!" exclaimed the monster.
"Is it true? I just can't tell.
For although I'm good at eating things,
I do not count so well."

"Let us count these things together,"
Said the genie, "and you'll see—
The <u>dish</u> is **1**, the <u>box</u> is **2**,
And then the <u>truck</u> makes **3**."
"**3** things! You're right," the monster said,
"Now what am I to do?
I've used up my **3** wishes
And I'm very hungry, too!"

"Gee, that's too bad," the genie said,
"But now my job's complete."
"I'm so *hungry*," said the monster,
"Oh, I need something to *eat!*"

"I'm sad your wish for cookies
Can't come true," the genie said.
"That's okay," replied the monster........

"...I'll just eat the truck instead!"

And as the monster ate the truck,
The genie disappeared,
Saying, "I have seen a lot of things—
But boy...is *that* guy weird!"

Cookie Monster's Colored Candy Cookies

Oh, boy! Me got a good one for you this time! COLORED CANDY COOKIES! They not only *delicious*, they *beautiful*, too! For this one you need:

1. Your COOKIE DOUGH! If you no have some in icebox, make some QUICK! (See Volume 1.)

2. Some lollipops or hard candies. Find some pretty colored ones.

3. Hammer (or something to break up candies with).

4. Tin foil.

Cover cookie sheet with tin foil. Sprinkle flour on cloth. Roll out dough on cloth (about ¼ inch thick) and cut into thin strips. Now use strips of dough to make pictures on tin foil, like this . . .

Now break up colored candies into little pieces and put pieces in openings in your pictures, like this . . .

Have a grownup heat oven to 400 degrees. Now bake 6 to 8 minutes. While me wait, me play Roosevelt Franklin's favorite game. Hmmm. Me look around, and guess what me found. It something RED and...TASTY—

COOK BOOK!

REMEMBER! Never use oven without grown-up helping you.

O.K. COOKIES READY!

If you want to make beautiful COOKIE-POPS, put sticks in while still hot. Then let cool and peel off tin foil when hard. Oh, they ALMOST too pretty to eat.

But not quite!

The Count's Counting Page

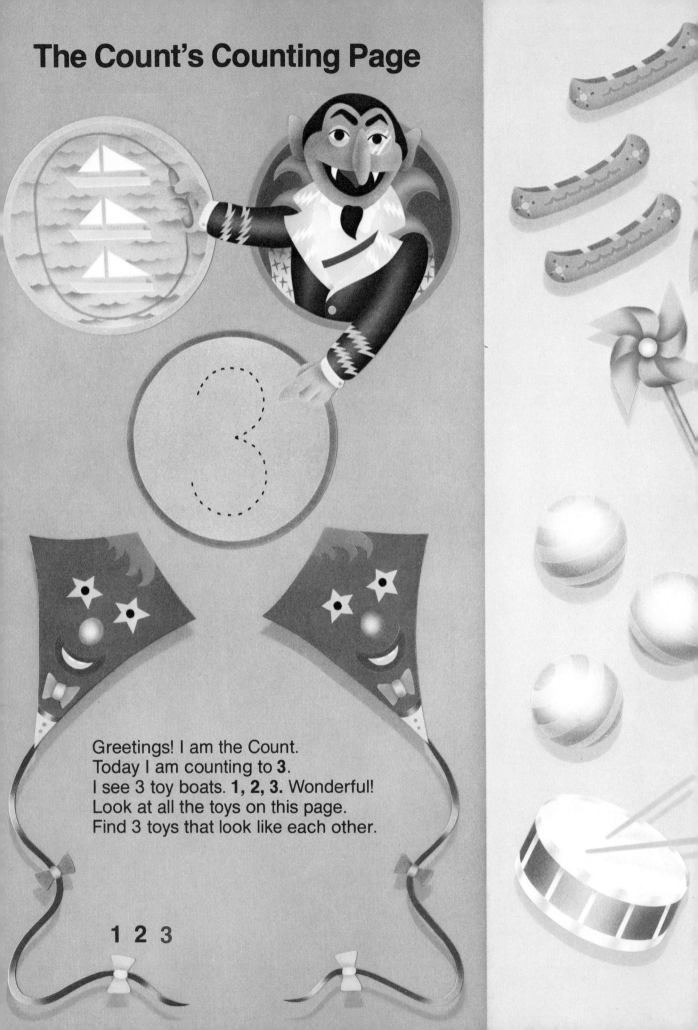

Greetings! I am the Count.
Today I am counting to **3**.
I see 3 toy boats. **1, 2, 3.** Wonderful!
Look at all the toys on this page.
Find 3 toys that look like each other.

1 2 3

Art-so-fine

RUB-A-DUB-DUB

Rub-a-dub-dub,
Three men in a tub,
And who do you think they be?
The butcher, the baker,
The candlestick maker;
Turn 'em out, knaves all three!

AROUND THE CLOCK WITH GROVER

 **8** o'clock.

I am wearing my nice warm bathrobe.
It is time for breakfast.
Today I am having some crispy
crunchy cereal with milk.
What do you eat for breakfast?
Touch the picture of me eating breakfast.

 **10** o'clock.

I am playing outside with Betty Lou and Ernie.
It is a little bit cold,
so I am wearing my red sweater.
Touch the picture of me playing outside
with Ernie and Betty Lou.

 **12** o'clock.

Lunchtime.
I always eat lunch with my mommy.
Today we are having
peanut-butter-and-banana sandwiches.
What time do you eat lunch?
Touch the picture of us eating lunch.

 **4** o'clock.

I am going to the store.
Touch the picture of me going to the store.

 **6** o'clock.

Dinnertime.
Oh, yummy!
Carrots and tomatoes and
brussels sprouts and chicken.
What do you eat for dinner?
Touch the picture of me eating dinner.

 **8** o'clock.

Time for bed.
I am a *very* tired monster!
I am wearing my fuzzy green pajamas.
What do *your* pajamas look like?
Touch the picture of me going to bed.
Nighty-night!

A B C

F G H

L M N O

S T U

Y Z 1 2

6 7